DRAKE PUBLIC LIBRARY
115 Drake Avenue
Centerville, IA 52544

FAST FACTS

SOCCER

Tom Palmer

SEA-TO-SEA
Mankato Collingwood London

This edition first published in 2012 by

Sea-to-Sea Publications
Distributed by Black Rabbit Books
P.O. Box 3263, Mankato, Minnesota 56002

Copyright © Sea-to-Sea Publications 2012

Printed in China

All rights reserved.

9 8 7 6 5 4 3 2

Published by arrangement with the Watts Publishing Group Ltd, London.

Library of Congress Cataloging-in-Publication Data

Palmer, Tom.
  Soccer / by Tom Palmer.
     p. cm. -- (Fast facts)
  Includes index.
  ISBN 978-1-59771-330-6 (library binding)
  1. Soccer--Juvenile literature. I. Title.
  GV943.25.P35 2012
  796.334--dc22
                              2011001214

Series editor: Adrian Cole
Art director: Jonathan Hair
Design: Blue Paw Design
Picture research: Sophie Hartley
Consultants: Fiona M. Collins and Philippa Hunt, Roehampton University, UK

Acknowledgments:

AFP/Getty Images: 28. Barker/Hulton Archive/Getty Images: 18. Andrew Barker/Shutterstock: 7. Fethi Belaid/AFP/Getty Images: 20 inset. Bettmann/Corbis: 14. Clive Brunskill/Getty Images: 12. Linda Bucklin/Shutterstock: 25. Joao Luiz Bulcao/Corbis: 22-23. Dennis Doyle/Getty Images: 20-21. Gallo Images/Getty Images: 19t. Alexander Hassenstein/Bongarts/Getty Images: 16. Hoang Dinh Nam/AFP/Getty Images: 24. Wolfgang Kumm/Corbis: 15. Steve McMay/ABACA/PAI: front cover. Damien Meyer/AFP/Getty Images: 13. Anne Christine Poujoulat/AFP/Getty Images: 6. Stephane Reix/For Picture/Corbis: 17. Reuters/Corbis: 27. Clive Rose/Getty Images: 8. Vladimir Rys/Bongarts/Getty Images: 1, 10. Antonio Scorza/AFP/Getty Images: 22 inset. Srdjan Suki/epa/Corbis: 11. Michael Steele/Getty Images: 5. Bob Thomas/Popperfoto/Getty Images: 9, 19b, 26, 29. Wang Daiwei©Fotoe/Link PL: 4. Every attempt has been made to clear copyright. Should there be any inadvertent omission please apply to the publisher for rectification.

February 2011
RD/6000006415/001

Every effort has been made by the Publishers to ensure that the web sites in this book contain no inappropriate or offensive material. However, because of the nature of the Internet, it is impossible to guarantee that the contents of these sites will not be altered. We strongly advise that Internet access is supervised by a responsible adult.

Contents

What Is Soccer?	**4**
Soccer Field	**6**
Go Professional	**8**
Women's Game	**10**
Europe's Greatest Teams	**12**
FIFA World Cup	**14**
Soccer Records	**18**
Soccer Rich List	**20**
Different Games	**22**
Soccer Fitness	**24**
The Original 12	**26**
Who's Best?	**28**
Answers	**30**
Glossary	**31**
Index	**32**

Words that are highlighted can be found in the glossary.

What Is Soccer?

The modern, international **game we know as soccer has come a long way from its early days.**

Modern-day Cuju festival.

The first known sport that was anything like soccer was called Cuju. Cuju was played in China in the second century and involved kicking balls stuffed with feathers.

Modern-day mob soccer festival.

Early soccer in **medieval** Europe was called mob soccer. Whole villages fought to get the ball to each others' marketplaces—there were no other rules!

FF Top Fact

Main rules of modern soccer:
• two teams of 11 players play for 90 minutes, which is split into two 45-minute halves
• the teams try to score more goals than each other by getting the ball into the other team's goal.

 How many footballs can you find on the pages of this book?

Soccer Field

Soccer is played on a field no more than 130 yards (120 m) long and 100 yards (90 m) wide. Each team defends their half of the field and attacks their opponent's half.

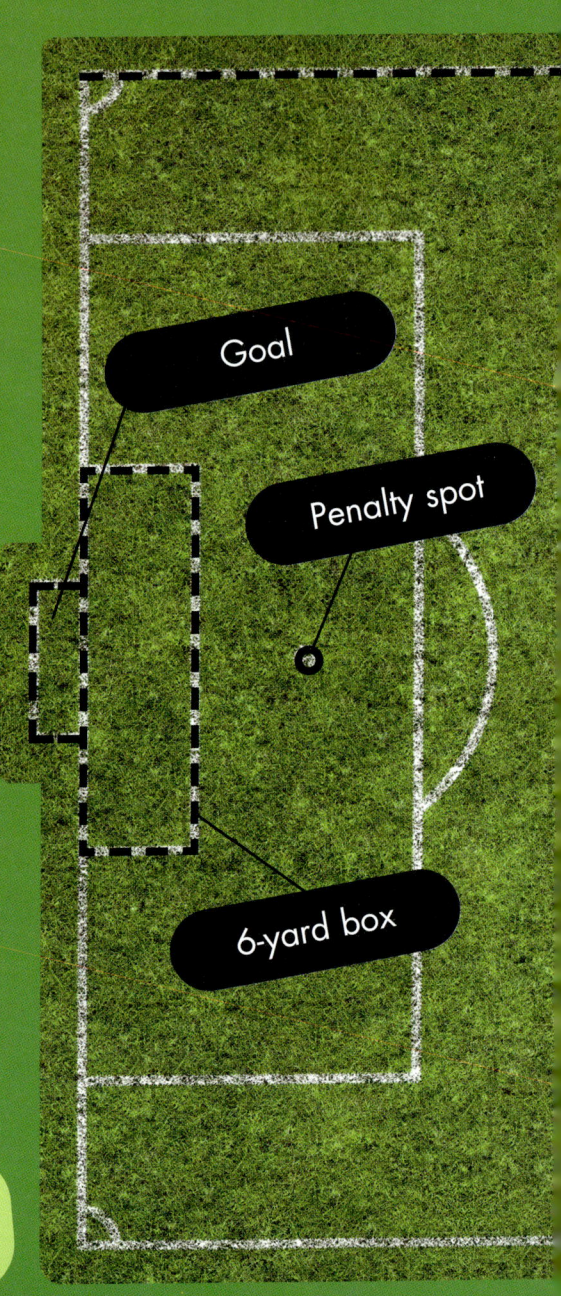

Goal

Penalty spot

6-yard box

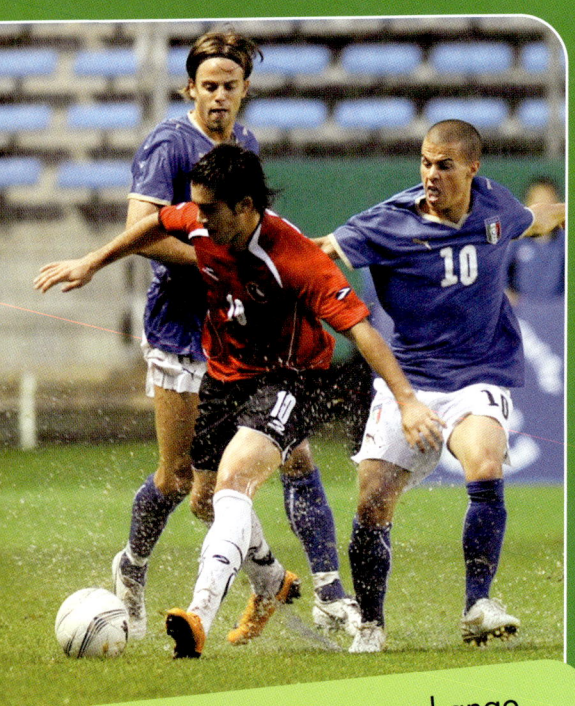

Field conditions can change during rain and other weather.

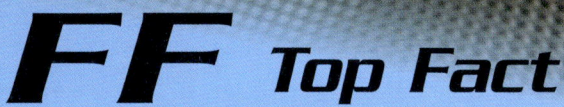

FF Top Fact

The soccer field is known in the official rules as "the field of play."

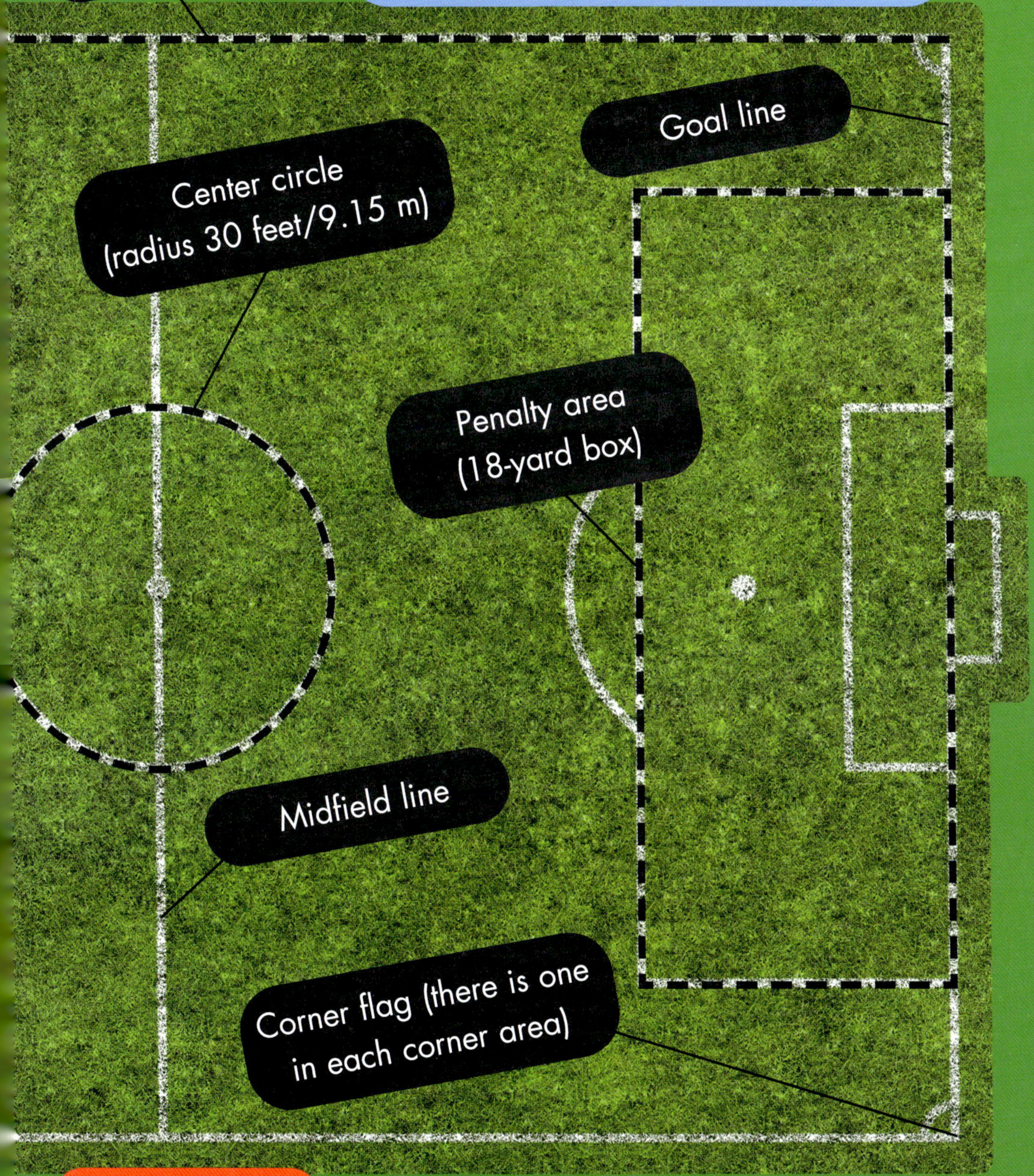

- Sideline
- Goal line
- Center circle (radius 30 feet/9.15 m)
- Penalty area (18-yard box)
- Midfield line
- Corner flag (there is one in each corner area)

ONLINE//:

http://www.fifa.com
Visit the FIFA web site and type "classic stadiums" into the search line to find out more about the **classic** stadiums of the world.

Go Professional

It takes a lot of skill and hard work to become a professional soccer player. Many players don't make it, but these five steps might help. Who knows? Maybe someone reading this book will become a professional player.

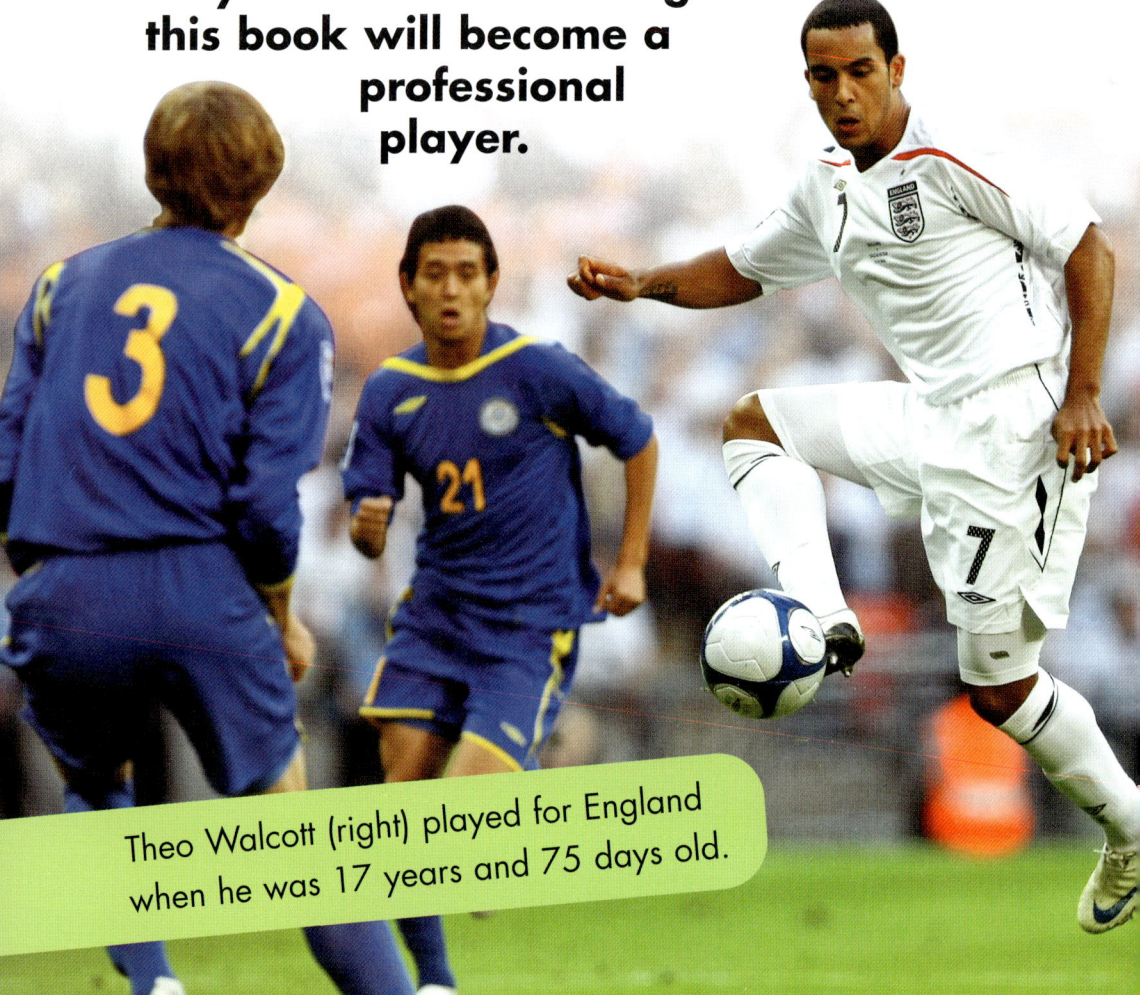

Theo Walcott (right) played for England when he was 17 years and 75 days old.

1. Play soccer as often as you can—with friends or family, or on your own.

2. Join a local team. If you need advice in finding a good one, try the AYSO: www.soccer.org.

3. Make sure you get support from your parents or carers.

4. Once you're in a team, work hard but also enjoy yourself.

5. Eat a balanced diet and stay healthy.

FF Top Fact

Norman Whiteside (above, left) was the youngest soccerer to play in a World Cup finals match. He was 17 years and 41 days old when he played for Northern Ireland on June 17, 1982.

ONLINE//:

http://www.fifa.com Visit this web site of the Fédération Internationale de Soccer Association (FIFA). Select your country from the "associations" menu and find out more about clubs in your area.

Women's Game

Women's soccer is more popular than ever. Hundreds of new teams are being formed every year.

The top international women's team is the USA. Many female players in the United States are professional, so they can train and play soccer every day. Brazil, Germany, and Sweden also have successful women's teams.

> **?** Why do you think women's soccer was banned from 1921–1971?

FF Record

Arsenal are the best women's soccer team in England. They have won 12 out of 16 **league championships**.

FF Top Fact

Germany won the 2009 women's European Championship. They beat England 6–2.

ONLINE//:

http://www.ussoccer.com
This is the web site of the U.S. Soccer Federation, featuring women's team news, photos, and videos. Also features the men's soccer team.

Europe's Greatest Teams

Twelve teams have won the Champions League (or European Cup) more than once. Teams from Spain, Italy, and England have dominated **the tournament since it began in 1955.**

In 2001 Liverpool won three competitions: the Champions League, the FA Cup, and the League (Premier) Cup.

Real Madrid's Ruud van Nistelrooy forces through toward the goal.

Fast Facts Winners

Champions League winners

Teams	Wins	Teams	Wins
Real Madrid	9	Manchester United	3
AC Milan	7	Inter Milan	3
Liverpool	5	Benfica	2
Ajax Amsterdam	4	FC Porto	2
Bayern Munich	4	Juventus	2
Barcelona	3	Nottingham Forest	2

ONLINE//:

http://www.uefa.com/uefachampionsleague/index.html
Visit these UEFA web pages for the Champions League to learn all about the League's history, statistics, clubs, and current standings.

FIFA World Cup

The World Cup is the ultimate soccer tournament. It takes place every four years. Countries from **six** continents **play one another to qualify, with most teams coming from Europe and South America.**

FF Top Fact

Brazil is the only team to win the World Cup when it has been held outside their own continent: 1958 (above) in Europe and 2002 in Japan. No European team has ever won the tournament away from Europe.

Marco Materazzi of Italy heads the ball toward the goal during the 2006 World Cup Final.

Countries qualify for the World Cup finals by playing other teams from their part of the world. Teams that have qualified go to the World Cup finals.

204 countries entered to take part in the 2010 World Cup. When the finals took place, only 30 teams were left.

The current World Cup trophy is the second trophy to be used. Brazil was given the original Jules Rimet trophy to keep after winning the tournament for the third time in 1970. A new trophy was introduced in 1974 and it is still used today.

FF Record

Only eight countries have ever won the trophy. Brazil have won it the most times: five.

Fast Facts Winners

World Cup winners

1930	Uruguay
1934	Italy
1938	Italy
1950	Uruguay
1954	West Germany
1958	Brazil
1962	Brazil
1966	England
1970	Brazil
1974	West Germany
1978	Argentina
1982	Italy
1986	Argentina
1990	West Germany
1994	Brazil
1998	France
2002	Brazil
2006	Italy
2010	Spain

The current World Cup trophy weighs 14 pounds (6.2 kg) and is 14 inches (35 cm) tall.

 The World Cup is played every four years. Why wasn't it played between 1938 and 1950?

ONLINE//:

http://www.fifa.com/worldcup/index.html
Find out more about the World Cup, including its history, photos, team lists, and statistics.

Soccer Records

The first soccer club formed in Sheffield, in England, in 1857. Since then records have been set and broken, including: highest scores; biggest attendances; and most international appearances.

These are some of the most amazing records. Choose below from answer A, B, or C. The actual answers are on page 30—no cheating!

1. Dixie Dean scored the most goals in one season in English soccer. (Everton, 1927–1928). In 39 games, how many goals did he score?
A: 40, B: 50, or C: 60

2. Egypt have won the final of the Africa Cup of Nations more than any other team. But how many times? A: 3, B: 7, or C: 9

3. The 1950 Brazil–Uruguay World Cup final had the world's biggest attendance at a soccer game. How many people were there? A: 104,113, B: 154,915, or C: 199,850

ONLINE//:

http://www.fifa.com/worldcup/archive/germany2006/index.html   Watch archive videos of highlights from the 2006 World Cup games in Germany.

Soccer Rich List

For most fans, soccer is simply about seeing their team winning. But soccer is a multimillion dollar business.

Top soccer clubs can earn hundreds of millions of dollars through ticket income, shirt sales, and selling rights to TV and sponsors.

Every year a company named Deloitte publishes a list of the richest soccer clubs in the world. It tells you how much each club earns.

Fast Facts Rich List

The top five in 2010:

1	Real Madrid	$533.86 million
2	Barcelona	$407.41 million
3	Manchester United	$364.1 million
4	Bayern Munich	$322.35 million
5	Arsenal	$218.85 million

FF Top Fact

Real Madrid's Bernabeu stadium (shown here) holds 80,000 people.

ONLINE//:

http://www.realmadrid.com
Homepage of the richest soccer club in the world: Real Madrid. Catch up with the latest team news, photos, and videos.

Different Games

Around the world there are many other ways soccer is played.

Beach soccer is more than just a group of friends playing at the seashore. It has its own rules, which include players not wearing shoes. Beach soccer is famous as the sport where Brazilian players become so skillful.

Futsal is an indoor version of five-a-side soccer. There are no walls or boards at the side of the field, as in some five-a-side versions of the game. The ball is smaller than a normal soccer ball and has less bounce.

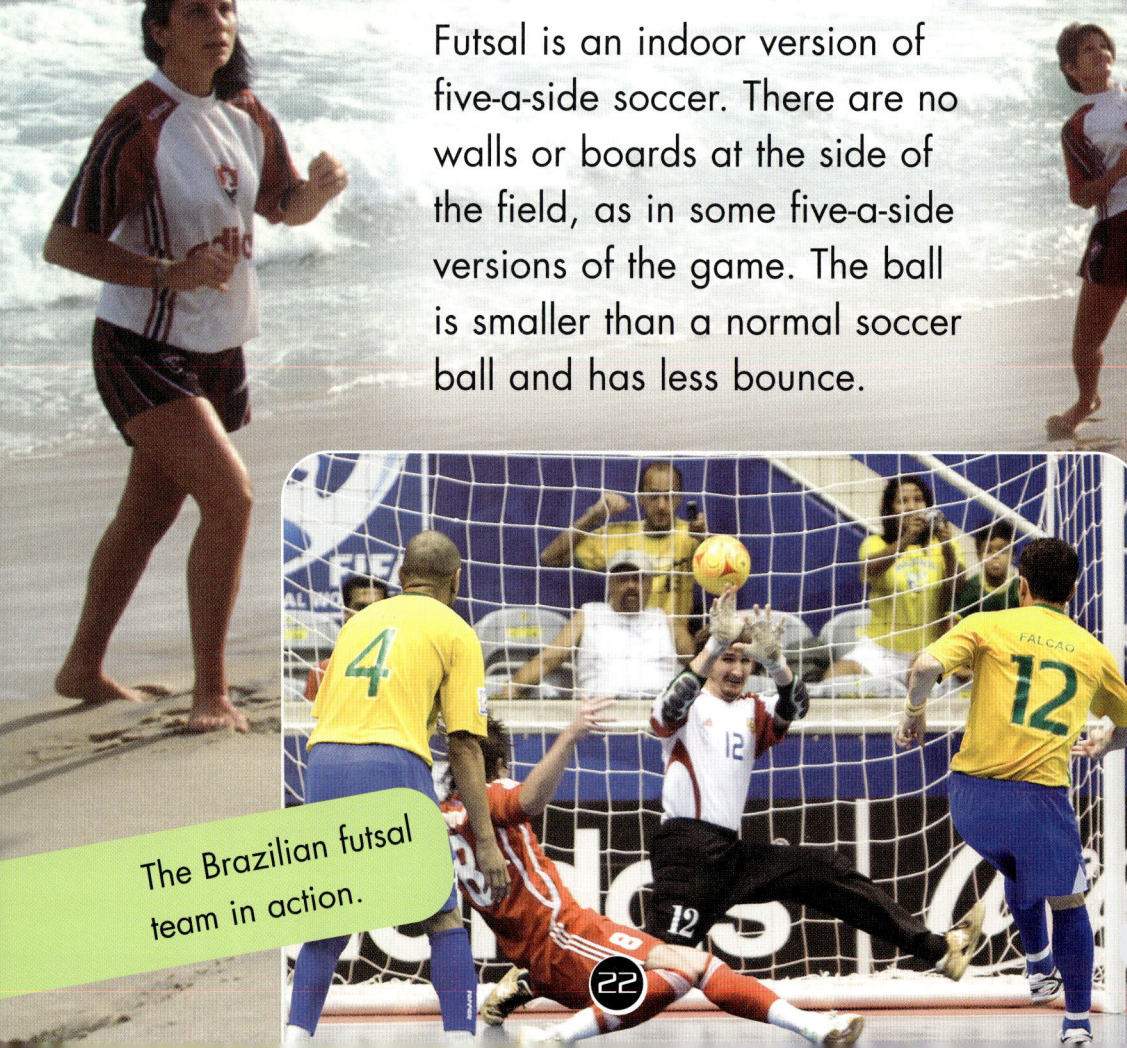

The Brazilian futsal team in action.

These girls are beach-soccer training in Rio de Janeiro, Brazil.

Power soccer is played by two teams of four people in wheelchairs. The players use footguards to kick the larger-than-normal ball up and down the field. Power soccer has its own world cup.

ONLINE//:

http://www.fipfa.org/   IPFA is an independent federation of National Organizations governing power soccer clubs in their separate countries. Find out about the clubs and leagues, and get up-to-date news.

Soccer Fitness

As well as training and staying in top shape, soccer players must eat well and live a healthy lifestyle.

Amateur and professional players often have diet sheets. These show the players what they should and should not eat. Players are encouraged to drink water regularly and not to smoke or drink alcohol.

A player's professional career may only last 10–15 years. It is important to stay in shape, especially as players get older, so they can play at the top level.

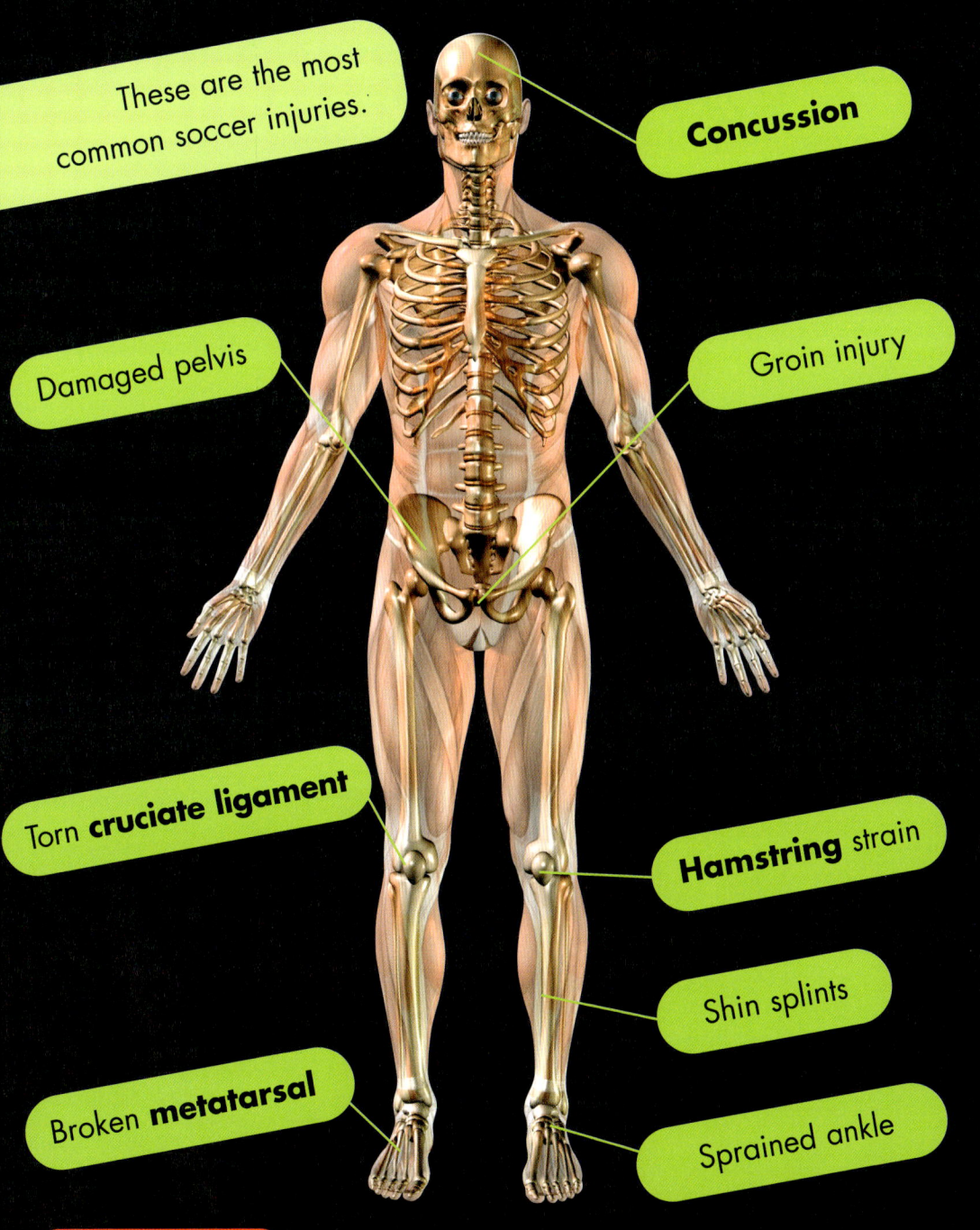

These are the most common soccer injuries.

Concussion

Damaged pelvis

Groin injury

Torn **cruciate ligament**

Hamstring strain

Shin splints

Broken **metatarsal**

Sprained ankle

ONLINE//:

http://www.mypyramid.gov/guidelines/index.html
Find out everything you need to know about dietary guidelines for the best diet to follow to keep yourself in top shape for playing soccer.

The Original 12

Twelve clubs have the honor of being the original **founding members of the English soccer league in 1888. But where were they in 2010–2011?**

Premiership
Aston Villa, Blackburn Rovers, Bolton Wanderers, Everton, Stoke, West Bromwich Albion, Wolverhampton Wanderers.

Championship
Derby County, Burnley, Preston North End.

League One
Notts County.

League Two
Accrington Stanley.

This is the Aston Villa team that won the FA Cup in 1913.

FF Top Fact

Of the original 12 teams, Everton has been the most successful winning the league title nine times. Aston Villa has won it seven times.

Wolverhampton Wanderers was promoted to the Premiership in 2009.

 Do you know which of the 12 clubs is the oldest? Search online (see below) to find out which team won the first English Championship.

ONLINE//:

http://www.nationalfootballmuseum.com
Web site of the National **Football** Museum, where you can find out how soccer **jerseys** have changed, and follow a key dates timeline.

Who's Best?

Two people are usually considered the best soccer players ever: Pelé, of Brazil, and Diego Maradona, from Argentina.

There is little to tell them apart. They shared the FIFA Soccer Player of the Century award. The experts can't agree who is the best, some choose Pelé, others choose Maradona.

Pelé in action in 1960.

Why don't you decide for yourself?
Here are some statistics about their careers:

	Pelé (Brazil)	**Maradona** (Argentina)
Age at national **debut**	16	16
Club games	468	590
Club goals	501	331
National games	92	91
National goals	77	34
World Cup wins	3	1
Club trophies	25	10

Maradona lifts the World Cup in 1986.

? Some people think Maradona does not deserve to be called the best soccer player because he has been banned for taking drugs. What do you think?

Answers

Page 5: There are 16 footballs shown in the pictures throughout this book.

Page 10: The soccer authorities at the time believed that women were better off at home, where they could take care of their families.

Page 17: World War II (1939–1945) meant that soccer could not be played.

Pages 18 and 19: 1=C, 2=B, 3=C.

Page 27: Preston North End is the oldest of the clubs.

Page 29: The answer to this question will depend on your own opinion. Try discussing the question with your friends to find out what they think.

Glossary

Amateur—not professional. In soccer this means a player has another job because he or she does not get paid for playing soccer.

Classic—something that is considered to be a great example and very important.

Concussion—the effects on the body after being knocked out.

Continent—one of the seven large land areas in the world.

Cruciate ligament—cross-shaped band in the knee.

Debut—the first time something or someone appears in a particular place.

Dominated—to have been the most successful at something for a period of time.

Football—the name given to soccer in many parts of the world, especially in the UK.

Hamstring—a tendon at the back of the knee.

International—something that occurs worldwide.

Jersey—the team shirts worn by soccer players and other sportspeople. Fans can buy them to show which team they support. In the UK, a team's identifying clothing is called a "strip."

League championships—a type of competition in which teams play against each other. Scores are recorded in tables.

Medieval—relating to the period of history called the Middle Ages (c. 476 A.D. to 1453).

Metatarsal—any of the five long bones in the foot.

Original—the first, or earliest to exist.

Professional—not amateur. In soccer this means that players are paid to play soccer, so they can spend their time practicing their skills.

Qualify—in soccer, to be entered into a competition after winning specific soccer matches.

Index

A, B
Argentina 17, 28, 29
Arsenal 11, 21
balanced diet 9, 24, 25
beach soccer 22, 23
Brazil 10, 14, 16, 17, 19, 22, 23, 28, 29

C, D
Champions League 12, 13
Cuju 4
Dean, Dixie 18

E, F
Egypt 19
England 8, 11, 12, 17, 18, 26–27
English clubs 1888 26–27
European Championship 11
field 6–7
fitness 9, 24–25
FA Cup 12, 26
FIFA 7, 9, 28
FIFA World Cup 9, 14–17, 19, 29
futsal 22

G, I
Germany 10, 11, 17, 19
injuries 25
Italy 12, 15, 17

L, M, N
league championships 11
Liverpool 12, 13
Maradona, Diego 28, 29
Materazzi, Marco 15
mob soccer 5
Nistelrooy, Ruud van 13
Northern Ireland 9

P, R
Pélé 28, 29
power soccer 23
Real Madrid 13, 21
rules 5

S, T
soccer clubs 20–21
Spain 12, 17
Sweden 10
training 8, 9, 24

U, W
UEFA 13
Uruguay 17, 19
USA 10, 11
Walcott, Theo 8
Whiteside, Norman 9
women's soccer 10–11, 30